THE VALKYRIE'S DREAM

DREAM

THE PARANORMAL COUNCIL #14

LAURA GREENWOOD

Visit Laura Greenwood's website at:

www.authorlauragreenwood.co.uk

Cover by Ammonia Book Covers

The Viper's Dream is a work of fiction. Names, characters, places, and incidents are the products of the author's imagination or are used fictitiously. Any resemblance to actual persons, living or dead, businesses, companies, events, or locales is entirely coincidental.

If you find an error, you can report it via my website. Please note that my books are written in British English: https://www.authorlauragreenwood.co.uk/p/report-error.html

To keep up to date with new releases, sales, and other updates, you can join my mailing list via my website or The Paranormal Council Reader Group on Facebook.

Parts of The Viper's Dream were previously published as the short story, Snakes and Ladders. They have been significantly changed since then.

Contents

BLURB

When Autumn's Father encourages her to marry a man she doesn't want to, she does the only thing she can think of and runs away.

Nate has lived his whole life knowing he's an anomaly even in the paranormal world. Born a snake and made into a human by his genie Father, he's surprised when he feels the mating bond.

After Autumn's hand is forced, the new bond between them is tested to the limit and it'll take everything they have to convince Autumn's family that she should choose her mate.

-

The Viper's Dream is part of the Paranormal Council series and is Autumn and Nate's complete story.

CHAPTER 1

AUTUMN

A utumn hoisted herself over the sill of her bedroom window, and over onto the desk she'd placed there purposefully for this reason. It wasn't the quickest way into the house, but it was the best one when she wasn't supposed to be out of it. Despite being in her mid-twenties, her father still liked to think he could boss her around.

Unfortunately, according to dryad customs, he could. And that was without taking into account the fact that she was tethered to one of the giant willow trees in the garden.

Maybe she shouldn't have been sneaking out, but it was the only way she could do her work and earn her own money so one day she'd be able to show everyone that she was more than just the spoiled daughter of rich parents.

"Where have you been?"

Autumn jumped as her father's voice boomed through the room.

"Out," she responded. He didn't need to know she'd technically been breaking into someone's house. He wouldn't understand that she was only doing it to retrieve stolen magical items in the first place. And she wasn't about to tell him. He'd probably try and ground her for life. Whether for the breaking and entering, or for sneaking out of their mansion in the first place, she wasn't sure.

"Where?"

"With friends," she answered, hating how good the lies sounded.

"Really, Autumn? Most of your friends were at the ball tonight. Like you should have been."

Shit. That wasn't good. She'd not forgotten about the ball, she'd decided not to go to avoid another night of being bored half to death by the elite paranormals who frequented them. All the forced politeness and uncomfortable clothing only added to the torture, especially when she wasn't like her parents. She didn't want political power, nor did she want to sit on the Nymph Council in the future. She wanted a life of adventure and not knowing what was around the corner. But that wasn't possible for dryads, or other types of nymph. Their tethers restricted their movements too much.

"Your brother was there too. With his mate."

Double shit. Ever since Felix had brought his mate home, their parents had been getting on about when Autumn would find her own, and settle down to have children. Basically, everything she didn't want. Apparently, it didn't matter to them that finding her fated mate was basically down to chance.

"I was busy," she muttered, not looking her father in the eye. He could sense a lie from her, she was sure. Though that could just be an echo of childhood making her think that.

"You can't just skip out on important functions. We have a reputation to uphold, and I won't have Aaron Dentro thinking I can't control my children. First Felix mating with a witch, and now you, doing whatever you are."

"You love Mia," she pointed out, hating the way he was talking about her sister-in-law. And it was true, they did love Mia, they had done from the moment Felix brought her home.

"Yes, but she's not a dryad."

"Neither is Xylia Dentro's mate," Autumn pointed out, proud of herself for actually remembering that, even if she couldn't remember exactly what the man was. There'd been a certain amount of muttering when the two of them had gotten married about five years ago, which was always welcome for breaking up the monotony of life.

"That's not the point, Autumn." She could hear the shadow of anger in his voice, and if she'd been a weaker woman, she might have trembled. She was used to her father though, and he was all threat, with no actual bite. He wouldn't do anything to her. She was his little girl after all.

"But Daddy..."

"Stop," he commanded. Oh no, this wasn't going to go as well as she hoped then. "I need to decide what to do with you." He motioned for her to move away from the window, and she left reluctantly.

She hated being made to feel like she was some snotty teenager again, and every now and again, he managed to do just that. She knew he loved her, and they had a good relationship, other than right this second, and the whole Autumn having to go to balls bits. But he didn't see her as an actual woman. She was still a little girl.

He leaned forward and clicked the lock on the window, removing the key and pocketing it. Autumn almost laughed. If he thought that was her only way out of the house, he was delusional.

Rule one of what she did: always have an alternative escape route, sometimes her life might depend on it. Well, maybe not her life. She'd like to think the High Council would interfere before it got that far. But someone could call the human police and detain her.

"Good night, Autumn, I'll talk to you in the morning."

Ominous, but it would give her time to prepare for what was to come. Hopefully, she'd be able to convince him that she wasn't up to anything. Or that she deserved to have at least some freedom considering her age.

"Good night, Dad," she replied, smiling at him as sweetly as possible in an attempt to feign innocence.

The door clicked shut, and she sighed, flopping down onto her huge double bed. The soft mattress dipped beneath her and she stretched out. It was possibly too much for one person, but that was her family all over. Her father had made good money in the past few years, and he'd upgraded massively to show it off.

Reluctantly, she sat up again, knowing it was time to message the Boss and tell him her job was done, and that she was out of commission for a few days. Hopefully, he'd understand.

Complete. Dropped in the normal place. Out of town for a few days. She hit send.

Her phone chirped, and she glanced back down at her hand. Acknowledged.

She set it down and started to strip off her clothes. She was done for the night, and clearly trying to leave the house wouldn't be the wisest move.

Which was fine for now. She was tired anyway and it would be good to get some rest before she talked to her parents. Hopefully, it wouldn't be a long conversation.

Chapter 2

Nathair

Nathair caught his reflection in the mirror and stopped to examine himself, searching across his skin for the telltale flash of scales that would reveal his former self. Despite having lived with his family for nearly ten years, he still expected to see hints of his true nature shining through.

He shouldn't have a human form. But thanks to his adoptive father's genie magic, he was essentially a shifter, though it was impossible to know to what extent without genetic tests, which his father had been reluctant to pursue in case it became common knowledge that his son had once been the runt of a nest of vipers.

Most of the time, it wasn't something he thought about very much, but when his brother had come home saying he'd sensed the mating bond between two people, he'd started thinking about whether or not that was going to be something he could have himself. Not that he'd asked his parents about it. He didn't want them to think he wasn't grateful for the life they'd given him, especially when they'd treated him the same way they had their own son.

Seeing nothing out of the ordinary, he moved away from the mirror. He couldn't be late for work, especially when his employers lived in the more expensive part of town. The quality of care he gave to their gardens mattered a lot. While it might not have been the job his parents wanted for him, he enjoyed spending his time outside, no matter what the weather was like.

The walk to his first job of the day was a pleasant one, with the leaves of the trees shading his path seeming to be on the turn from summer to autumn. It was a little early, but nature had a way of making sure things happened the right way.

A large house rose up in front of him. From what he'd seen of the family, it was too big for them, but that wasn't his judgement call to make. Especially as he hadn't interacted with any of them very much since he started working there.

He set about tidying the banks of the stream next to the surprisingly young willow tree that was a little out of place compared to the rest of the garden. Maybe he was wrong about the tree. As much as he'd been able to study up on, he wasn't an expert in these things. But something about the tree called to him.

It didn't take him long to find a steady rhythm with his shears, snipping along the overgrown grass growing in tufts at the side of the stream. If it was up to him, he'd have left it, but that wasn't his choice.

After a while, a soft humming filled the air

He jumped, dropping his shears and narrowly missing his feet with them. It was a good job he'd invested in a sturdy pair of boots.

Nathair turned slowly, searching the surrounding area for where the noise was coming from. To his surprise, a young woman had approached the willow tree and leaned out to touch it, her hand brushing against the bark tenderly, as if she was interacting with someone she loved.

He stood still, transfixed by the woman and whatever it was she was doing. If only there was a way for him to get closer and find out. Maybe that was an invasion of her privacy, but she wasn't exactly hiding what she was doing.

Except that he did have a way to get closer. He didn't even need to strip off his clothing to do it, thanks to his brother, his clothes would change form with him. Just one advantage of Austen's genie magic.

He focused on his true form, and painlessly shifted into the small patterned snake he'd been born as. He wasn't particularly large like some of the snakes he'd seen since gaining his human form, but that had never bothered him. As the runt of his nest, he probably wouldn't have grown to a particularly large size anyway. If he'd managed to survive this long.

He slithered through the grass, feeling the short blades tickle against his scales as he did.

Knowing he wouldn't be able to see much of the woman from this angle, he used his agile form to twist himself around one of the drooping branches of the willow. His firm, muscular body clung tightly to the wood as he climbed until he was about his human height.

The woman was still standing with her hand pressed against the willow bark. There was something mesmerising about the way she was interacting with the tree, almost as if she was glowing.

Was she some kind of genie? He'd never met one who wasn't part of his family, but he'd always assumed it was only a matter of time before he did.

There was a beauty to her that had nothing to do with her pale skin and dark hair. He was fairly sure it was her connection to nature, though he had no idea how he knew that.

His mind started to drift as he continued to be hypnotised by her movements and he couldn't help but think about what it would be like if her hand was on his head.

"I should have known you'd be here," a male voice broke through the calm and Nathair's head swivelled around to study the tall man walking towards the tree.

He had the same dark hair as the woman, though Nathair's sharp eyes could make out a slight greying at his temples.

"I needed somewhere calm," the woman replied, her voice low and somewhat melodic.

"The house is calm," the older man replied.

"Hardly," she muttered under her breath, but Nathair's enhanced hearing could pick up on it.

"Autumn, you need to stop this." He almost seemed to stamp his foot, which was ridiculous, why would a grown man want to do that?

"Stop what, Dad?" She turned to look her father in the eye.

"The sulking."

"Then have them take the spells off the gate. Or Rylan to stop following me. I know he's there, I'm not a fool."

Nathair couldn't help but appreciate the way she was standing up for herself.

"He..."

"Is following me Dad. I know you asked him to, so get him to stop. I don't like being watched all the time."

Nathair flickered his tongue, trying to taste in the air where Rylan was hiding. He wasn't an unobservant person, so why hadn't he noticed there was another person about?

"He's..."

"Stop it, Dad," she demanded. "I know you've done it so I don't disappear off again."

"It's more than that."

Nathair watched as Autumn raised a questioning eyebrow, glad his vision was strong enough to pick it up.

"I want you to marry him," the older man said.

"What?" Autumn's voice rose several octaves as she questioned him.

"Marry, Autumn. It will give you some structure in your life, as well as someone who can keep an eye on you..."

Nathair could tell, even before the man had finished speaking that Autumn wasn't going to like that. She didn't exactly seem like the wilting flower needing protecting and sheltering.

"No."

"Something has to change, Autumn," he told his daughter.

Nathair hissed in response, completely involuntarily. He wasn't sure what was up with him.

"Fine, but not by getting married to Rylan," she insisted.

"If not him, then someone else," her father responded, a stern look on his face.

"I'm not getting married to anyone," she threw back at him.

"You will, Autumn, and that's final. I'll make the announcement tomorrow." The older man turned and walked away before Autumn could respond.

Nathair's heart skipped a beat. If the announcement was that she'd just marry someone, perhaps he'd be able to help her.

Autumn grunted and kicked the tree, before instantly smoothing her hand over the bark. "I'm sorry, I didn't mean it," she whispered to the tree, leaning in even closer.

Nathair continued to watch her, leaning further outwards and almost losing his grip on the branch he was wrapped around. He probably would have done if not for the tight coils of his body. Luckily, spending most of his time as a human hadn't seemed to inhibit his snake skills.

He watched the woman for a few moments more, before realising she wasn't going to do much more than stare at the tree. If he was going to help her, then he needed a better plan than staring from afar.

CHAPTER 3

AUTUMN

A utumn could have sworn there was someone watching her as she'd talked with her dad. And she didn't mean Rylan. He might do her dad's bidding, but had the foresight to disappear when necessary. Not that it mattered. He was probably fully aware of what her dad wanted her to do. He had a choice. Unlike her.

"Hello?" she called. It might not work, but it was worth trying just in case. The chances of someone who wasn't friendly getting past all her family's defences was unlikely.

A rustling came from the right, and she turned in that direction, surprised to find a small golden snake clinging to one of the branches of her willow tree. Surprise fluttered through her. She'd seen snakes around before, but none of them had ever looked like this.

"Hello," she repeated, softer this time, and reached out a hand towards the creature.

It shook its head.

A frown pulled at her face. She had to be seeing things, snakes didn't shake their heads unless they were part of children's books.

"Okay...how are you?" She had no idea what about the snake made her ask, but the question slipped out before she had too much time to examine it.

The snake stayed silent.

Autumn shook her head. Of course the snake was silent. It was a snake. She supposed it could be a shifter, but its small size made that seem unlikely. Unless it was a child. But again, that seemed unlikely. What shifter parents would let their child slither around in strange gardens. Actually, quite a lot of them probably would. She didn't understand much about shifter culture.

The snake untangled itself from the willow branch, and coiled itself on the floor. A haze of golden smoke seemed to rise from the creature.

She might not know a lot about snakes, but she definitely knew they shouldn't be doing that.

The haze faded away, leaving a man standing in front of her instead of the small snake. His hair and eyes shone like gold, drawing her to him in a way she hadn't expected. She'd never felt this way before. It was an almost kind of helpless feeling. Like she wasn't completely in control of herself.

And she hated it.

"Very well thank you," he replied, his voice smooth and velvety as it rolled over her.

Oh no, when had she turned into such a girl? She wanted thrill and adventure, not romance and seduction.

Though the seduction part could also be fun. She wondered if the snake-man still had a forked tongue in this body, but pushed those thoughts to the side. That wasn't the most pressing concern she had right now.

"How about you, Autumn?" he asked.

The way he said her name sent a small thrill through her, only for it to be replaced by a mix of confusion and concern.

"How do you know my name?"

He glanced in the direction of her house.

Ah. He'd been listening to her previous conversation.

"It's rude to eavesdrop."

"It wasn't done on purpose," he admitted. "I was tending to the garden." He gestured down the stream to where a bag of tools sat abandoned.

He wasn't lying, as far as she could tell, but perhaps he was just good at it. She knew he was a paranormal being of some kind, but he wasn't acting like any shifter she'd heard about before.

"Do you have a name?" she asked, deciding it would be easier to get answers if she was polite to him.

"Yes."

"Are you going to tell me?"

"Nathair," he answered softly.

His golden-brown eyes bored into her. She felt it through every part of her body, and wanted it more.

Against her bare skin, and looking into her soul.

This needed to stop. She wasn't this girl, and she'd never wanted to be this girl.

"Do people call you Nate?"

"You can call me whatever you'd like, Autumn," he responded, his smile growing larger.

"Okay, Nate it is." She liked it. It sounded good, and fell from her tongue easily. Almost like it was meant to be there.

Maybe it was, maybe this was her mate. But, no. She shouldn't be thinking like that. Mostly because her father was right in one respect. Having a mate, or a husband, or any kind of tether, would stop the life she wanted to lead from happening. The tree her life force was connected with was bad enough at times.

She valued her freedom And she wasn't willing to give it up for anything, even her fated mate.

"Are you going to say anything else?" she asked. "Only I have a lot of things to do and..."

"Do you really not want to get married?" he interrupted.

He was the first person to question what she actually wanted.

"Of course not, I want to live my life before getting married."

"What if you married me instead?" he blurted out, before covering his mouth.

She raised an eyebrow at him. "Go on." She had no idea what exactly he was going to propose, but at this point, she was willing to listen to just about anything if it got her out of going with her dad's choice. Whoever that was going to be was surely going to be insufferable.

"It wouldn't be a proper marriage, just in name only. You could do whatever you wish. I could do whatever I wish."

"You can try, but it's traditional for a dryad bride's father to be given gifts."

"I can bring gifts. What would he like?" Nate asked her instantly, a boyish gleam in his eyes. This was going to be far far too easy. If he succeeded in impressing her father, then he'd be allowed to marry her, and slipping away from the odd snake shifter would be far easier than from Rylan, whose stealth skills almost rivalled her own.

Almost. But not quite.

"I don't know yet, he'll announce it tomorrow," she said, a little dejected by that. She had no idea what her father would ask for. But given how he'd become in the last few years, there was little doubt in her mind that it would be outrageous, and likely out of Nate's range.

"Okay, whatever it is, I'll get it and bring it to him. Then you'll be able to marry me." He gave her a stunning smile, and she returned it weakly.

This day had been a strange one, and she wasn't sure what to make of it. Only time would tell.

CHAPTER 4

NATHAIR

N erves assailed him as Nathair took in the opulence of the house. Up until now, he hadn't had any reason to be inside, and could count the number of times he'd passed the threshold on one hand.

Maybe he should have accepted Austen's offer to come with him after all. But his brother hadn't seemed keen on Nathair's plan to find out what gift Autumn's father wanted in order to secure her hand in marriage.

His gaze flitted to the woman he'd come here for. Her lips were pursed and she kept glaring at her father. That made sense, she'd already expressed her distaste for the whole situation.

None of the other men seemed to have noticed how she was feeling, they were more intent on winning the prize.

"Thank you all for coming," Autumn's father said from his place beside her. "My daughter, Autumn, wishes to invoke the old ways, and have her hand decided by the giving of a gift."

The man next to threw Autumn a long look when he didn't think she was watching. Her frustrated expression deepened and turned into a scowl.

Maybe Nathair stood a chance at winning her heart as well as helping her avoid marrying someone she didn't want to.

"Tradition dictates three gifts," her father continued. "If any of you can bring me a cake made from an asp's milk, and a solid gold apple, then I will inform you of the final gift. If, and only *if* you succeed in all three, you will win my daughter's hand in marriage. If not, it will be forfeited to Rylan Firr."

He wished he could talk to Autumn and reassure her that he was going to help her get out of this situation. Though her face said it all. She didn't want to be sold off to the highest bidder. He needed to make sure she was okay with him trying to find the gifts before he did so. The last thing he wanted to do was insult her or make her uncomfortable.

There was a low rumble around the room as the small crowd of men moved towards the exit. Nathair was surprised by how many of them there were, though perhaps he shouldn't be. Autumn was a beautiful woman, and judging from the house and grounds, her family were well off. Maybe they had a lot of power within the community.

He hung back and caught Autumn's eye. There was no way he was going to head out to find the gifts without talking to her first.

To his surprise, she smiled at him and gestured towards the gardens.

He gave a small nod and headed outside. He wasn't sure precisely *how* he knew where to go, but he found himself heading towards the willow tree where they'd first met.

Nathair shifted from one foot to the other as he waited for her to arrive. Maybe she was just toying with him?

He pushed the thought aside. As much as she clearly didn't like what was happening, she didn't seem like a cruel person.

"Hey." The moment her voice filled his ears, his heart skipped a beat.

"Hi," he responded.

"Thank you for coming today." She reached out a hand and touched the trunk of the willow tree. He wanted to ask her what was so special about it, but this wasn't the time for that.

"I said I would."

"I know."

He paused. "Are you okay?"

She sighed. "Yes and no. I'm fine, but this is all..."

"Messed up?" he offered.

She let out a sharp laugh. "That's one way of putting it. I've always known Dad liked the old ways, but I never expected him to put me through them. Most nymphs let themselves fall in love or find their mate before they get married."

"You're a nymph?" He glanced at the stream, wondering if that was her tether.

She nodded. "Well, a dryad. But that's a kind of nymph."

"It is?"

"Of plants." She reached out and touched the tree again.

Understanding dawned on him. She was affectionate towards the willow because it was part of her.

"Are you worried about managing to get the gifts?" she asked. "I can probably help with the golden apple, but I might struggle with the cake."

He shook his head. "I don't think either will be a problem."

She frowned. "You don't seem very worried about it."

"I'm not."

"But they're not supposed to be easy challenges. Even witches would struggle with the cake."

"I'm not a witch."

"I know."

He could tell she wanted to ask him more, but didn't dare. Or she thought it was rude to. He wouldn't mind, though it was best if he didn't reveal his family were genies and that was how he planned to get ahold of the items he needed.

"Do you know what the last gift is?" he asked. If he could get a head start on that, he might stand a chance.

"I'm sorry, Nate, I have no idea."

His name, even a shortened version, sent a pleasant shiver down his spine. Something about the way she said it only deepened the determination within her. He couldn't deny that he was drawn to Autumn in a way he'd never been drawn to anyone before, though he had no idea why.

"It doesn't matter, I'll make sure to get that one too."

She gave him an appraising look, as if trying to make sense of how he was so confident. "Why are you doing this?"

"I don't know," he admitted.

Autumn raised an eyebrow.

"Not what you expected?"

She chuckled, a warm sound that he wanted to hear more of.

"I think I was expecting some kind of reasoning that you found me the most beautiful woman in the world, or some other nonsense like that." She wrinkled her nose as if to express distaste.

"I do think you're beautiful." Maybe he shouldn't have said that given her dislike of it, but it seemed better to be honest about it all. "But that's not why I want to help you."

"Then why?"

"I can't explain it. There's just something that makes me feel like I should. Like we're connected."

"I know what you mean," she whispered.

Surprise raced through him. He hadn't expected her to say that, or anything along those lines. It was reassuring to know she understood.

"What does it mean?" he asked.

"I'm not sure. But I know who I can ask to find out," she said. "If I find an answer I'll tell you."

"Thanks, I'd like that."

A genuine smile crossed her face. "Good luck with the gift finding. If I can help, let me know."

"I will," he promised, knowing he wouldn't have to. He'd have the gifts sorted before the end of the week, then he could present them to her father and find out what the final one was. After that, it would just be a case of sorting out the details of the wedding, but he figured he'd leave that to Autumn. She'd probably want a long engagement so the two of them could get to know one another properly.

He didn't mind the sound of that himself. Somehow, he knew that she was going to be his future, even if he didn't have an explanation about why. Hopefully, she'd be able to find out the reason, but until then, he was going to do everything he could to make sure she didn't have to marry someone she didn't want to. Even if that meant technically making it so she'd marry him.

Chapter 5

Autumn

"Autumn, please?" Rylan begged.

She hated it when he acted like this. Almost as if he wasn't the bad guy in the situation. It seemed to have escaped his notice that he was trying to trap her into marriage.

Autumn turned to face him again, finding him appraising her adoringly.

There really wasn't anything wrong with Rylan. A lot of women would probably be thrilled to have his attention to themselves. But she wasn't one of them. She hated being told what to do more than anything, and Rylan was as guilty as her father for trying to do that.

"No," she said firmly. It was a shame this was going to end up ruining what was left of their friendship.

"All you have to do is say yes to marrying me, and your father will stop his marriage contest."

"Gods, Rylan, what's wrong with you?"

He sucked in a deep breath, probably disliking being called out.

"I just want you to be happy," he protested, a conflicted look flitting across his face.

"Then stop insisting on this stupid marriage farce." What didn't he understand about the situation? She didn't want to get married and he was trying to force her into it.

"You think I have a choice?" he half-shouted. "I'm as pushed into this as you are, Autumn. Don't get me wrong, I like you. A lot. But that doesn't mean I don't care what you want."

"Then why haven't you stopped it?" She seethed inside. At least Nathair had been honest about his intentions towards her, and at this point was seeming like a much better choice for her than Rylan. Even if she barely knew him, he seemed to be at least trying to respect her choices.

"When the choice is me or some other random guy you don't know? Did you meet any of the men who were here the other day?"

He really should stop talking.

"Leave."

"But..."

"Leave, Rylan."

"He's not leaving, the gift-giving is about to start," her father said as he entered the room.

Autumn scowled at him. The fact he didn't see anything wrong with selling her off to the highest bidder was a major problem as far as she was concerned. She needed to get Felix to come home so he could talk some sense into the rest of her family.

"Is anyone even here for it?" Rylan asked, disbelief in his voice. So he'd made the assumption that none of the men would be able to produce what her father had asked for. That was typical. What was the point in setting a challenge no one could win?

Probably so they knew who she'd end up with.

"Yes, two men."

Autumn's heart skipped a beat.

Had Nathair really managed to find what her father wanted? He'd seemed so confident about his abilities, but she hadn't been completely convinced. Not because she didn't think he was competent, but because she knew how hard it would be to find them.

She glanced at the men in the room with her, unsurprised to find them conversing in a hushed tone that left her out of the conversation. It seemed like neither of them had learned that the best way to get her to agree to whatever plan they had was to actually talk to her about it.

While she was frustrated by their actions, it left her free to make her way over to the doorway and peer around it. As her father said, there were two men waiting nervously in the other room.

One of them turned, revealing his golden features.

Relief crashed through her. Nathair had come through with her.

He must have spotted her watching him, as he waved.

She smiled and returned the gesture.

"I see you're excited," her father said jovially, making her jump by patting her on the back.

She didn't respond. How could she when she didn't have the words to?

"Let's get this over with," Rylan muttered, pushing past them both to get into the hallway.

Her father followed suit, leaving Autumn to trail after the two men. She supposed she could run off, but there was a small part of her that was curious about what would happen next. So long as she didn't have to get married here and now, she'd be fine.

"Good evening," her father said, smiling widely as he moved past her and out into the hall, beaming at the men assembled there. No wonder he was happy. People were playing the game by his rules.

Her father made his way towards the two men, and she noticed Nathair puff out his chest in pride.

She didn't recognise the other man, but that didn't stop him from producing a golden apple for her father's approval.

Her father took the apple and lifted it to his mouth. Despite her anger, Autumn stifled a giggle. She could feel the life force emanating from the fruit, and knew her father wouldn't suffer any consequences from ingesting it. As if on cue, he took a deep bite, and she heard a satisfying crunch.

Her father dropped the apple to the floor and crushed it under his boot.

For a moment, the man looked as if he might come up with an excuse for why he hadn't provided what her father wanted, but he seemed to think better of it and raced out of the room, leaving her life for good.

Not that it bothered her too much. He hadn't even taken the time to introduce himself to her.

Confidently, Nate held the apple out for her father.

Even from this distance, she could tell that this one was solid gold. It felt different to her than the one that had come from a tree.

"And the cake made of asp's milk?" her father asked.

"Of course." Nathair held out a small wrapped package.

Her father took it, but didn't open it. She had no idea what the cake would be like, but it didn't sound particularly appetising. Perhaps her father didn't want to try it and find out.

"Well done," her father said, a small hint of resignation in his voice.

"What is the third item you'd like me to retrieve for you?" Nathair asked.

Surprise flitted across her father's face. Had he been so confident that no one would be able to find both a golden apple and a cake made of asp's milk that he hadn't even planned the third item? That sounded likely, especially with how much he wanted Autumn to end up with Rylan.

"You must retrieve the diadem of Rosalind," her father said decisively.

Autumn's eyes widened. How was that going to be possible? The last she knew, the diadem had been locked away in a museum for years, wrongly labelled as an item of pagan worship.

"I shall do as you wish," Nate said, bowing his head. He turned to her. "Autumn."

Her heart fluttered.

She gestured in the direction of the willow tree, hoping he'd understand that she wanted him to meet her there. She needed to find out what help he needed to find the diadem so she could give it to him. She would much rather he won this silly competition rather than ending up with Rylan by default.

Hopefully, between the two of them, they'd be able to come up with a solution.

CHAPTER 6

NATHAIR

N athair paced back and forth while he waited for Autumn to arrive at what seemed to be their official meeting place.

He resisted the urge to shift back into his snake form just in case Autumn's father turned up instead. He didn't imagine the man would be very pleased to learn that Nathair was meeting his daughter. Especially not when it seemed that they were in cahoots with one another.

He only relaxed once he spotted her hurrying over to him with a harried expression on her face.

"I'm so sorry, I didn't think it would take so long for me to get away," she said.

Just like the other times she'd been by the willow tree, she reached out and touched the trunk. He liked that she seemed so connected to it, even if he didn't fully understand it.

"I haven't been waiting long," he assured her.

Autumn raised an eyebrow. "You realise I know when you left the building, right?"

"I forgot."

"Thank you for getting the apple and the cake," she said softly. "I appreciate you coming through for me like that."

The way she spoke made it clear that she didn't think he'd be able to get the diadem her father had asked him for.

"You're welcome."

Something hung in the air between them. He longed to reach out and touch her, but didn't want to rush her, especially when she seemed so against getting married or any other kind of relationship.

"So, the diadem," she said.

"I can get it."

"How?" She didn't do much to hide the surprise in her voice.

"I have my ways."

"That's not good enough." She crossed her arms across her chest and fixed him with a stern expression. "If you want me to trust you enough to think you're a better choice than ending up with Rylan, then you're going to have to start telling me stuff."

Indecision warred within him. Something deep inside told him that he could trust this woman with everything, but he didn't know where that urge came from or what it actually meant.

"Genie magic," he said, deciding that the truth was probably the best.

"You have a genie?"

At least she wasn't denying their existence. He'd heard of that happening sometimes.

"Not exactly."

Autumn didn't say anything. She must be waiting for him to provide more of an explanation. He didn't really blame her. He'd probably want more in her position too.

"Shall we sit down?" he suggested. "Then I'll tell you the whole story."

Surprise flitted across her face. "Sure."

She sat down on the bank of the small stream and patted the ground.

He took it as an invitation and sat next to her. Despite the fact they weren't touching, and that they were meeting in broad daylight, it was strangely intimate. He liked it more than he was ready to admit.

"I'm not a shifter."

"But I saw you turn into a snake," she countered.

"I know. But that was the form I was born with. I was the runt of the nest and was struggling to survive. I was found by a genie and given this form." He gestured to himself to illustrate his point.

"I didn't think that was possible."

"Genie magic is some of the most powerful in the world. I don't think just any genie could do it, but Dad can."

"Dad? You're losing me."

"He adopted me after he used his magic on me. He and his wife raised me along with their own son. They live not far from here."

"And that's how you managed to make the golden apple and the cake from asp's milk appear," she said, seeming to have worked it out.

"Yes. My brother, Austen, made them for me with his magic. I was going to ask him to do the same with the diadem." It seemed simple as far as he was concerned. It had worked for the two previous items, it should be enough for the diadem.

"I don't think that's going to work," Autumn said.

"Why not? Your father didn't find an issue with the previous gifts, did he?"

"No, not at all. He can't find any fault with them. But you knew that was going to be the case, didn't you?"

He nodded. "But why won't it be the same with the diadem?"

"Because he wants a specific one. You can't just make a different one and expect it to pass his inspection. It needs to be *the* diadem."

"Hmm. I can see how that might pose a bit more of a problem," he admitted. "I could just ask Austen to retrieve it with his magic."

"I don't think that'll work either," she admitted as she plucked at a few blades of grass. "But it might be worth a try."

"You sound as if you know how I can get it."

She bit her bottom lip. "It depends how you feel about breaking some rules."

"Whose rules?"

"Everyone's."

He chuckled. "My start in life broke nature's rules. I think I can handle some rule-breaking."

Autumn chuckled. "You might want some time to think about this first."

"I'm intrigued."

"The diadem is in a museum. That's why Dad picked it, he wanted to make it too hard so you wouldn't complete it."

"Sneaky."

"He's just desperate for me to marry Rylan." Her lip curled up in distaste.

"You don't like him?"

"Right now, no," she muttered. "Normally he's fine. It's just when he's become obsessed with obtaining me that things started to become a problem."

"I can see how." He paused, not really wanting to ask whether or not he was doing the same.

Autumn stopped plucking at the grass and reached out to take his hand in hers.

"You're doing things differently."

"Am I, though?"

She laughed sharply. "I suppose this wasn't quite what I had in mind when I thought about meeting someone. But I realise that you're doing it from a good place."

"I don't know why I'm doing it," he admitted.

"I think you do. It's the same reason I'm letting you." She said the words so softly that he wasn't too sure whether he really heard her.

Neither of them said the word, but it seemed they were both thinking it. There was a reason they were being pulled together and it was a force far stronger than any set of tasks to prove he was worthy of marrying her.

"So, the diadem?" he prompted after they'd been silent for a little too long.

"I have a plan, but it involves a little bit of breaking and entering. Can you do any genie magic?" she asked.

He shook his head. "All I can do is shift into a snake."

"Still useful," she mused. "If you want to take part. I can try and get it on my own if you'd prefer."

"No, I'll come with you."

"Thanks, I appreciate it. Meet me here tomorrow night."

"Do you need me to do anything to prepare?" he asked.

She thought for a moment, a pensive expression flitting across her face. "No, I don't think so. But if you give me your number, I'll message you if that changes."

He nodded and pulled his phone out of his pocket, handing it over so she could connect the two of them.

"There, all done." She handed it back to him. "I look forward to stealing the diadem with you."

"Me too." Surprisingly, he meant it.

CHAPTER 7

AUTUMN

S he wasn't sure what made her send Nathair a message to ask him to meet her, especially as she hadn't heard back from her contact about the diadem yet. It was hard to make a plan when she didn't have all the information.

And yet here she was, standing by her willow tree waiting for him to arrive. She'd never been this interested in spending time with someone before. Especially not someone she'd just met.

Maybe it was better if she didn't think too hard about what it might mean, especially when she wasn't sure she'd like the answer.

But there had to be a reason she was okay with him competing for her hand in marriage. Even the thought of everyone else taking part in this ridiculous farce of a competition was enough to have anger rising within her, but Nathair felt different.

A small hiss drew her attention to the willow branches in front of her.

Autumn let out a surprised laugh at the small golden snake twirled amongst the leaves. Without thinking too hard about it, she held out her hand. After a moment's hesitation, he uncurled himself and slipped onto her arm.

Was it weird for her to have a living man on her arm? Considering it was the first time she'd ended up in this situation, she had no way of being able to tell.

She took the chance to study Nathair's serpent form in more detail. His scales were several different shades, all of them complementing the others perfectly.

She rubbed his head, being careful not to get caught on the small horns which protruded up from them. She didn't think they'd be poisonous, but she also didn't want to make him uncomfortable.

His forked tongue flicked out of his mouth, tickling her skin. He followed it with a hiss which she took to be her cue to set him down on the ground so he could shift back into his human form.

Autumn crouched down and touched her hand to the grass, letting Nathair slither off. She stepped back and waited as a cloud of purple smoke surrounded him.

Now that she knew the truth, it was easy to see the differences between Nathair and a shifter. They didn't have the magic around them when they shifted, and there was something about the way he felt that was different too. It was subtle, and if she hadn't known about his origins, then she'd never have thought to pay attention long enough to notice.

No wonder he'd managed to hide his true nature for as long as he had.

Nathair stood straight and brushed off his jacket.

"How do you shift with your clothes on?" she asked. As far as she knew, it wasn't possible for normal shifters.

He shrugged. "I've always been able to. Are you disappointed by that?"

Her eyes widened at the implication. "No."

He raised an eyebrow, clearly not believing her. Maybe he had good reason not to. A small flutter in her belly at the thought of him naked was hard to ignore.

"I'd be disappointed if the positions were reversed." He winked at her, which only made the fluttering worse.

"Most people would be," she responded in an attempt to cover up the thoughts flooding through her head.

"Especially Rylan."

She scowled. "Don't talk to me about that traitor."

"You don't like him?"

"I do and I don't." She sighed and sat down on the bank of the stream.

Nathair didn't wait to copy. They were close enough that even a small movement would be enough for them to touch, but the gap between them still felt like it was too much.

"We used to be friends. I've known him my whole life. But something changed a few years ago, especially after my brother found his mate." The fluttering reached new heights as she said the word, despite the fact she wasn't talking about herself. She'd never had a reaction like this to the idea of finding her fated mate before.

"What does your brother have to do with things?"

Autumn sighed. "How much do you know about nymphs and dryads?"

"Next to nothing. I've not known many paranormals in my life."

She snorted. "Other than the rarest."

A small smile played at the corner of his lips, only serving to cause small twinkles in his eyes. "I doubt genies are the rarest."

"They're not exactly common," she pointed out. "So my point still stands."

"As does mine. I've never known a nymph or dryad as well as I know you. I don't even know what the difference is."

"It's like fingers and thumbs."

"Ah, so all nymphs are dryads but not all dryads are nymphs," he said.

"Yes, but it's the other way around. Dryads are nymphs who are connected to plants." She reached out to touch a dangling branch of the willow tree. "There are other nymphs who are connected to other things found in nature. Streams, oceans, rocks, you name it."

He nodded. "I see. What does this have to do with Rylan?"

Autumn sighed. A small part of her didn't want to get into the nuances of her relationship with the other dryad, but Nathair was going above and beyond to help her, he deserved to know the full story.

"You don't have to tell me," he said quickly, presumably sensing her discomfort.

"Thanks, but it might help to talk about it. I haven't really had anyone to do that with." She suspected she could have reached out to Felix, but he'd been living away from the community ever since moving into his mate's house.

"Okay. Well just stop if you want to."

She flashed him a grateful smile. Why was this man who was almost a stranger being nicer about the situation than the people who were related to her and living in the same house? It didn't make much sense on either of their parts.

But now the idea of talking to someone about the situation had been raised, she wanted it.

"Nymphs are still very traditional. A lot of parents make marriage arrangements for their children, though not normally as elaborately as Dad is."

"That would be a very full social calendar otherwise."

She snorted. "You're not wrong. Thankfully, the community isn't huge, otherwise, there'd be a wedding a week."

"But with unwilling participants?"

"Less than there used to be. A lot of parents have started taking their children's preferences into account."

"But not all."

"No. And I seem to have drawn the short straw in that."

"Because of your brother?"

She nodded. "Felix met his fated mate."

"That doesn't sound like a bad thing," Nathair said.

"It's not. I've never seen him so happy, and Mia is lovely. But she's not a nymph."

Interest crossed Nathair's face. "So your mate doesn't have to be the same species as you?"

"No. It seems that they're more commonly a different one. I assume for genetic diversity or something like that. Why?"

For a moment, she thought he was going to say something about them. Though where she'd gotten that idea from, she had no idea.

"I'm the only one of my kind. I've always worried having a mate wasn't something I'd be able to do." He avoided looking at her.

"Oh." Disappointment welled up within her, but she pushed it aside, unsure where it had come from and not wanting to spend too long trying to work it out. That would likely lead her down a path she wasn't ready to go down. "Anyway, while the community as a whole is pleased he's found his mate, there's also a bit of a stigma against inter-species mates from the nymphs. I think Dad wants to offset that by having me marry someone deemed appropriate by the community."

"But what happens if *you* find your mate?" he asked.

She let out a pained sigh. "That's not likely."

"Your brother did."

"He was lucky. Finding your mate is hard. And it's even harder when you can't leave one place for very long. I'm tethered to my tree, I can't spend more than a couple of days somewhere else or I'll start to get sick. When the only people who live around here are the other nymphs and dryads I've known my entire life, the chances of me meeting my fated mate is low." Her gaze slipped to him without her meaning it to him.

She still couldn't explain the pull she felt towards him. Or why she was telling him all of this. She'd never talked to anyone about her worries of never finding her mate before, and she hadn't intended to change that. But something about Nathair made him easy to talk to, and like she *wanted* to share all of her secrets.

"Can I ask you something?"

"Of course," he answered instantly.

"Why did you show yourself to me the other day? And why are you doing this?"

"That's two questions." From the way he said it, she had no doubt that he was teasing.

"I already answered more than two of yours," she responded in the same tone.

"That's fair. But I told you about where I came from already."

"In which case, you can ask me more questions in return."

"Deal." Nathair chuckled, a throaty sound that sent a pleasant shiver right through her. "The honest answer is that I don't know. Something just felt right about showing myself to you. And as for helping you with the marriage competition stuff, it's not completely selfless. I wanted to get to know you more and it seemed like a good way." He shifted slightly so they were facing one another better.

Her gaze drifted to his lips as her thoughts drifted towards imagining what it would feel like if he kissed her.

Shock flooded through her. Why was she thinking about that?

"I'm sorry, was that too much?" he asked.

She shook her head. "No, I guess I'm just not used to people wanting to get to know the real me, just the perfectly cultivated image my family makes me put out into the world."

"How do you know I want the real you?" He cocked his head to the side.

"I can tell," she whispered. "There's just something about you." She felt herself leaning in, but was incapable of stopping it even if she wanted to.

Which she didn't.

Anything to get closer to him.

Nathair reached out and tucked a stray strand of hair behind her ear. She bit her bottom lip, drawing his gaze to her mouth. From the hooded look in his eyes, she could tell he wanted this as much as she did.

"Kiss me," she whispered.

Thankfully, he didn't need asking twice. He closed the distance between them and pressed his lips against hers.

Her whole body tingled and she wrapped her arms around his neck, pushing her body against his as she deepened the kiss.

He wasn't the first man she'd kissed, far from it, but there was something about this that felt different. Like there was something deeper between them.

She didn't have long to think about it as he nipped at her bottom lip with his teeth and all rational thought fled. If she wasn't careful, they'd end up doing far more than kissing underneath her willow tree.

Not that she was opposed to that.

"Autumn?" her father called out across the grounds.

The two of them pulled away from one another and froze, neither of them sure what to do next.

"Autumn, I know you're out here," her father called again.

"Shift," she whispered to Nathair. "I don't know what he'll do if he sees you."

For a moment, she thought he was going to argue, but then he shifted back into his snake form and slithered up her tree.

She watched him go with a pang of regret travelling through her. "I'll message you," she promised, hoping he could still hear her.

A soft hiss responded, assuring her that he had.

With a deep sigh, she turned in the direction of her father's voice, leaving her tree and the man who had made her feel more deeply than ever behind.

For now.

Next time, they wouldn't be interrupted, she'd make sure of it.

CHAPTER 8

NATHAIR

H e tossed and turned, trying to get to sleep, but failing miserably. All he could think about was Autumn and how much trouble she was in and how much they needed to do in order to stop her from falling victim to a forced marriage.

He didn't even know what he was going to do once they had the diadem. It felt wrong to try and save her from one forced marriage just to make her go through with another one. He might want to get to know her, and their kiss may have been electric, but the last thing he wanted was to make her resent him by forcing a wedding.

A knock pulled Nathair from his thoughts. He sat up, letting the sheets pool around his waist.

"Come in," he called.

The door creaked open to reveal Austin standing on the other side with a concerned expression on his face. "I can hear you trying to sleep from the other side of the wall," his brother said dryly.

Nathair grimaced. "Sorry."

"Want to tell me what's bothering you?" Austin came into the room and sat down on the end of the bed.

Nathair sighed. He'd been doing his best to keep his family out of this, but it seemed like he had no choice but to finally talk about it.

"You know I asked you to make me that apple and cake?"

"Believe it or not, I can remember last week, yes." Amusement danced in the genie's tone, but Nathair chose to ignore it. "Are you going to tell me what that's about?"

Nate launched into an explanation, leaving nothing out, including the way he felt when he was around Autumn, and the kiss they'd shared.

Austin let out a low whistle once he was done. "Well that explains a lot."

"It does?"

He nodded. "It sounds like you might have found your mate."

Nathair blinked a few times. "I didn't think that was possible for me."

Austin shrugged. "Dad said he never knew for sure, I guess he does now."

"Maybe. We have no way of knowing how true it is." Hope welled up within him. He'd always dreamed of having a mate, but had tried to remind himself of how unlikely it was that he'd find one.

And it explained a lot about the way he felt when he was around the dryad.

"But how do I avoid losing her? If I make her marry me, it's only going to end badly."

Austin chuckled. "You're not wrong there. Look at how much Dad complains about his past masters."

"So what do I do? How can I stop her from resenting me if I get the diadem for her?"

"Well for one, it sounds like you'll be getting it together, right?"

He nodded.

"And you want to give her the right to choose her own husband? Even though you're mates?"

"Of course. I don't even know if we are mates, that's just a theory. But even if the universe says that we're well suited to one another, that doesn't mean she shouldn't get a choice in the matter, especially when it's something she's already bothered about."

Austin held his hands up. "Hey, I'm just asking."

Nathair sighed. "It's an impossible situation, I know that."

"I don't think it's as impossible as you think it is. You said that bringing the diadem is what means you win her hand in marriage, right?"

"Mmhmm."

"Then it's simple. Make sure she's the one that has the diadem. It's not like she can marry herself, right?"

"What if her father makes the argument that she didn't do the first part of the task?"

"Then her father is a bit of an ass," Austin pointed out.

"You're not wrong there," Nathair muttered. "But I can still see it being a potential issue."

"Then all you have to do is make sure she *has* done the first part." Austin held out his hand and let a haze of magic rise from it. A golden apple came into being on his palm, not unlike the one Nathair had taken to Autumn's father.

His brother handed it to him and then proceeded to summon a cake made of asp's milk in the same way.

"These tasks seem ridiculous, by the way," he said.

"I don't disagree. Autumn thinks her father is trying to make it so she marries the guy of his choosing by default."

"Then it sounds like you need to get her away from there sooner rather than later. Do I need to ask our parents to set up a room here for the two of you?"

Nathair sighed. "No. We don't know how she's going to feel about any of this. Maybe she'll want to use her freedom to travel the world or something."

Austin chuckled. "All right, it was just a suggestion."

"Thanks for your help."

"Any time. We're family, and that's what we do for one another."

Warmth spread through Nathair at the reassurance. He knew how his family felt about him, but it was always nice to have a reminder of that.

"Can you do that thing you used to when we were kids?" Nathair asked.

Austin frowned. "To send you to sleep?"

He nodded.

"I thought you didn't like the dreams it caused."

"I don't, but it's better than not sleeping at all."

"Hmm." Austin didn't seem convinced.

"Please?"

"All right. Lie back."

He shuffled back under the covers.

Austin reached out and placed a hand on Nathair's head. His skin tingled as the magic took hold and seeped into his mind.

The world disappeared and sleep took hold, along with a barrage of vivid dreams. It was hard to keep up with what was going on in them, the only thing that kept coming up in them was a clock tower. He didn't recognise it, but there must be a reason it was featuring so heavily.

If he remembered when he woke up, he would have to look it up and see if it was a real place.

CHAPTER 9

AUTUMN

E ven with everyone assembled doing their best to avoid any potentially awkward topics, the atmosphere around the dinner table was tense. Not that Autumn expected any different.

"Did you hear that Dad decided it's time for me to be married?" she announced.

Her brother frowned and turned to their father with a disapproving expression on his face. "What about her fated mate?" Felix asked.

"What about my *choice?*" Autumn tried not to let her anger seep through her words, but it was hard when her family were making it so hard.

"I was getting to that," Felix muttered.

"It's time she was married. People are starting to talk," her father responded.

She dropped her fork, letting it clatter against the dish. "No one is talking about anything," she insisted.

"That's what you think. But maybe if you'd thought about attending a council meeting every now and again, you'd hear differently," her father chided.

Anger mounted within Autumn, making her want to scream from the top of her lungs. How was this her life?

She pushed her chair away from the table and got to her feet. "Seeing as my opinion isn't needed, I'll just leave you to talk about me behind my back like everyone else apparently does."

Without waiting for anyone to respond, she hurried towards the exit, intent on heading down to her willow tree so she could soak in the comfort it would provide. Maybe she should consider going somewhere none of her family would think to find her, but what was the point in that? They'd just hunt her down.

The wet grass tickled against her bare legs, but she paid it no attention. A little bit of rain wasn't going to hurt her.

Autumn leaned her back against her tree and pulled her legs up to her chest.

It didn't take long for the telltale sound of someone following her to break through her thoughts. Surprise flitted through her as she recognised the dark hair and petite form of Felix's mate, rather than a member of her own family. Though technically, she supposed Mia was her sister-in-law.

"May I sit?" the witch asked.

"If you don't mind getting your dress wet."

"I can think of worse things I've been through," she joked, but a slight darkness in her voice said otherwise.

Autumn was well aware of what Mia and Felix had been through, she didn't need to rehash the details and put the other woman through it again.

"How are you feeling?" Mia asked.

"Like I'm up for auction and I don't even know who is bidding," Autumn muttered.

The witch snorted. "That seems about right. You know Felix will do everything he can to change your father's mind, right?"

Autumn let out a deep sigh. "I do. He's never been one for blindly accepting what father says."

"I'm glad to hear it. I don't want my kids to have to go through this."

"Are you..." she trailed off, realising it was probably rude to ask.

To her surprise, Mia laughed lightly. "Oh, definitely not. My niece is a handful enough as it is."

A smile spread over Autumn's face. "How is Fiona?"

"A menace, as always. Now she's discovered her ability to shift, she's become even more of a handful. If you think chasing after a child is bad, you should try playing hide and seek with a lion cub."

Despite her feelings, Autumn chuckled. "That sounds exhausting."

"You'd think, but I've never seen Bex happier than now she's found her mate again. Their family is complete, it's such a heartwarming thing to see."

The two of them lapsed into silence for a moment.

"How did you know Felix was your mate?" Autumn asked.

Mia tipped her head to the side with a curious expression on her face. "I thought you knew the story?"

"I do. But that's not what I want to know." She took a deep breath. "I was wondering what it felt like to meet your mate. How soon did you know? What did it feel like? Were there any magical tells?"

"That's a lot of questions," Mia said. "Is there a reason you're asking them?"

"Maybe," Autumn muttered.

The other woman smiled kindly. "I think I knew from the moment I met him. There was something about Felix that made me certain I could trust him with everything. I can't really explain it properly because it's not so much one singular emotion as things starting to slot into place."

"Ah."

"You've met them, haven't you?" Mia asked. "Your mate?"

Autumn sighed. "I'm not sure."

Mia raised an eyebrow.

"All right, I'm fairly sure he's the one. It's what you said, there's something about him that makes me certain I can trust him, even if I don't necessarily have any real reason to."

"Does he know about this ridiculous marriage competition?"

"He's in it," Autumn admitted. "But he's been talking to me about it first. It's not the same as the way father and Rylan are taking part in it."

"I see."

"I just don't know if he feels the same."

"If you're mates, then he will," Mia assured her. "And as for a magical tell, I think it depends on what kind of paranormal you are. I don't remember anything particularly noticeable from his side when I met Felix, but for witches, we let out a small spark when we first touch. It's a bit of a giveaway."

"And also handy," Autumn pointed out.

"Yes, unless you've already slipped someone the wrong love potion."

"Is that what happened? Felix always skipped over the part of the story that explained where your wedding date came from."

"Ah." Mia blushed furiously. "It turned out that my neighbour had been giving me a love potion for weeks running up to the wedding, to the point where I dosed him. It wasn't my finest moment. I've never used a love potion before. I was lucky that I met Felix the same day or it wouldn't have worn off."

"Autumn!" her father called out through the grounds.

She rolled her eyes. "He's been doing this more and more recently. I don't know why he doesn't just come to my tree when he wants to talk to me."

"Maybe he's forgotten *how* to talk to you," Mia said. "He might be struggling with his decision as much as you are."

"Maybe. But I'm still too angry about it to want to sit down and talk it through."

"Understandable. I would be in your position too," she admitted. "But once you're ready, I think the two of you should. There must be a reason he's decided to do this now. Maybe he's just trying to get your attention."

Autumn thought it was more likely that he needed an alliance with Rylan's family, and with Felix unavailable, his attention had fallen on her. Nymphs and dryads weren't particularly known for their romantic notions towards marriage. It was just as likely to come from love as it was to come from convenience.

"I should go see what he wants," she said, getting to her feet. "Thank you for talking to me."

"You're welcome," Mia responded. "If you need anything else, just message me. We can always meet up for coffee or something."

"Thanks, I appreciate it." She smiled and then headed back towards the house to find out what her father wanted. It was better to get it out of the way so he wouldn't bother her again.

"There you are," he said once he spotted her.

Autumn repressed the urge to roll her eyes. "You knew where I'd be."

"I've been thinking, this marriage competition is taking too long."

Her eyes widened. "If you hadn't made the requirements so hard, it would be over by now," she pointed out.

"The deadline is going to be brought forward until the day after tomorrow," he announced.

"No."

"You don't get a say in this, Autumn. If your suitor doesn't produce the diadem the day after tomorrow, then you will marry Rylan."

Instead of answering him and revealing *just* what she thought of his plan, she stalked off.

If there were only two days left to get the diadem, then that was exactly what she was going to do.

Anything to avoid marrying the way her father wanted her to.

CHAPTER 10

NATHAIR

Nathair approached Autumn's willow tree with a sense of dread settling in the pit of his stomach. He wasn't sure what was causing it, but something about the way he was feeling suggested that something wasn't right about the situation.

A shadowy figure leaned against the willow tree, filling him with hope that the way he was feeling didn't mean anything. She was waiting for him, just like she had been on the other occasions they'd met one another.

"Autumn," he called when he was close enough for her to hear.

"Not quite," a male voice responded. "I'm Felix."

"Her brother?"

The man chuckled. "Ah, so she does talk about me."

"She's mentioned you a few times," Nathair responded.

"And I'm guessing you're the man Autumn's been talking to my mate about," he responded.

Something perked up within him. "Autumn's been talking about me?"

"You're the one trying to win her hand in marriage, aren't you?"

Nathair approached the tree so he could see the man standing under it better. Even in the dim moonlight, he was able to see the resemblance between the two siblings.

"I actually want to win so she can choose for herself." The more he'd thought about his brother's idea for what he should do with the diadem, the more he liked it.

Felix's lips quirked into a smile. "She'll like that."

"I hope so."

A tense silence descended between them.

"Where is she? I half expected her to be here," Nathair said.

Felix sighed. "Gone."

A sharp pain travelled through him. "What do you mean gone?"

"She's gone," he repeated. "We don't know where. I assumed Dad said something to her that she didn't like and she took off."

He had to admit that did sound like Autumn.

"Do you know where I can find her?" he asked.

Felix shook his head. "I'm sorry, I don't. Mia, my mate, said she thought I should wait here in case you showed up. I don't know if you've met a witch before, but sometimes you just have to trust them."

"I haven't, but I'll keep that in mind for when I do."

"I'm sure you'll meet Mia sooner rather than later. She said my sister seemed very smitten with you."

"She did?" Excitement filled him.

Felix nodded. "Which means she'll probably tell you where she is if you ask. So long as you don't tell our Dad, I don't think it's going to be much of an issue."

"I don't plan on doing that," Nathair promised.

"Good. Then you should call Autumn and ask her where she is. It was nice to meet you."

"You too."

The two men nodded to one another, before Felix disappeared back towards the house.

Nathair waited until he thought he was out of earshot, and then waited some more just to be sure. He didn't think dryads had enhanced hearing, but he wasn't going to take any risks.

He pulled out his phone and scrolled to Autumn's contact number. He'd never called her before, only communicating via messages up until now. But if he wanted to find her, this was what he had to do. Especially as there was a chance that she didn't want him to find her.

To his surprise, it barely took two rings for her to answer.

"Nate?"

"Hey, Autumn."

"I didn't expect you to call."

"Your brother was waiting at your tree."

"Ah. Are you still there now?" she asked, the crackle of the line doing nothing to hide the music of her voice.

"I am, but I was just about to leave."

She paused as if thinking something through. "Will you bring me a branch?" she asked.

"Yes. But I don't know where you are."

She sighed. "I'll message you the address. Don't tell anyone."

"I have no intention of doing that," he promised. "Is there anything else you need me to bring?"

"No, I have everything else we'll need here."

"Need for what?"

"Breaking into a museum and retrieving the diadem," she responded as if it was the only logical answer. He supposed in some ways, that was true.

"Okay. I'll get your tree branch and bring it to you." It took him a moment to remember that she'd told him that she wasn't able to go far from her tree for long, but that having a small part of it with her would help prolong the amount of time she could spend away from it.

Just how long was the heist going to take? Her father had set a deadline and Nathair didn't think he was going to be particularly lenient if they were late.

"I'll be there as soon as I can."

"Thank you, Nathair." There was a pause as if she was going to say something else, but then didn't. "I'll see you soon."

"You too."

The line went dead, leaving him standing under her willow tree in the dark.

His phone lit up with a message, revealing the address of where she wanted him to go. He sighed with relief. A small part of him had expected her to still refuse to tell him anything and to do this alone. It was good to discover she meant what she said about them working together to solve the problems she was having with her father.

Carefully, he reached out and snapped a long branch of willow off the tree. It felt wrong to be doing it, but this was what she'd asked him for and he wasn't about to show up to meet her without it. Besides, the ease with which he'd managed to remove the branch almost made it seem like the tree itself was giving him permission to do it.

He curled it up gently, being careful not to snap it. At least he'd managed to take a more flexible part of the tree so he could do this. He slipped it into his pocket and turned to leave the tree and the mansion grounds behind.

A quick stop at his home to collect some supplies, and he'd be on his way to meet Autumn. If his brother was home, he might even be able to convince him to do a teleportation spell that would allow him to get there faster.

He hoped that would be the case. He didn't want to spend any longer without Autumn than he had to.

CHAPTER 11

AUTUMN

Autumn glanced over her shoulder, already worried that she'd left too much of a trail to follow. Maybe she shouldn't have sent the flat address to Nathair, it would make her too easy to find.

Except that she wanted to see him, and while she had some decent camouflaging abilities as a dryad, his small size while in his snake form would be able to give them the edge they needed while trying to retrieve the diadem.

Getting into the museum wasn't going to be an issue. She'd done it before. But that time, the item she'd been sent to retrieve hadn't been worth as much. Which meant more lax security and more time before someone noticed it was missing.

With the diadem, they'd be lucky to get an hour's head start on the people being sent to retrieve it. Which was probably why her father had set this as the final challenge to win her hand in marriage. He knew it would be too hard to pull off without getting caught.

The only thing he hadn't taken into account was Autumn's secret job in item retrieval. She was paid well because she was good at her job.

She turned the corner and made an abrupt stop in front of a rusty door. She reached out and rapped on it a couple of times.

A slot slid open, revealing a curious pair of eyes. "Password," the guard growled.

"Elderberry jam," she responded.

He grunted and closed the hatch so he could open the door. It swung open, revealing a dimly lit bar, complete with gambling tables and crowds of up-to-no-good paranormals. She was constantly surprised that the Paranormal Criminal Investigations department hadn't closed this place down yet, but maybe they realised there was a lot of use to be had from petty criminals.

"Is Desmond in?" she asked.

The doorman grunted and gestured in the direction of the bar.

Autumn rolled her eyes but headed over anyway. She'd never gotten much out of any of the workers here. They were paid handsomely to keep quiet and they took it seriously.

She hopped up onto the stool beside a man wearing a trench coat and a trilby hat tipped low over his face, obscuring it from view. She wasn't sure what the point of looking like he was up to no good was, but as far as she knew, Desmon had never been in trouble with the authorities, so it must work.

"What can I get you?" the bartender asked her.

"A rum and coke, and a whisky on the rocks for him." She gestured to Desmond, knowing that was how she'd get his attention.

"Coming right up." He pulled out two glasses and whipped up the drinks in a matter of minutes.

"Keep the change," she said, handing him enough money to cover the drinks and a healthy tip.

He nodded appreciatively and disappeared down the bar to tend to someone else.

"What do you want, Autumn?" Desmond asked, turning to her but not lifting his hat. She didn't think she'd ever properly seen his face.

"I need to know about the diadem of Rosalind and what kind of security I can expect around it." There was no point in beating around the bush. Especially here. No one in the room was up to any good, and while her missions were normally a little more morally sound than this one, she still wouldn't call what she did to make her living completely legal, especially with the amount of breaking and entering she normally ended up doing.

Desmond let out a low whistle. "That's a little above your normal wheelhouse."

"I still need the information," she responded.

"I'd leave it, if I were you. It's not worth the risk."

"I don't have that luxury. I just need information." She needed to stay firm or he wouldn't give in.

"Ah, you've finally got yourself into trouble stealing from the wrong person?"

"I don't steal, I retrieve," she pointed out.

"Give it a different word if you want, but you're a thief just like the rest of us."

She chewed on her bottom lip, but mostly because she understood why he said that, and why it was true. The thrill of getting caught and risking something serious was part of why she did it.

"Information," she said firmly.

"All right, fine. But if you get caught, you better keep my name out of it."

"Even if I didn't, I doubt Desmond is your real name," she muttered.

"Clever girl." He grabbed his whisky and swirled the glass around. The ice tapped against the sides of the glass, but he didn't take a drink. He'd probably be saving it for after she was gone. "It's not the worst thing you could want from the museum, but it's right in the middle of the main room. There are motion sensors and security guards."

"Armed?"

"No. They don't have a licence for that."

She nodded. It was one of the things that made her job a lot easier than some of her counterparts in other parts of the world.

"Any pressure sensors on the case itself?"

He shook his head. "As far as I know, they only have a couple of units built that way, and they both contain items far pricier than the diadem of Rosalind. You're lucky in that respect. But you're never going to get past the guards."

"You've said that before, and yet here I am."

"Maybe you're really good at talking yourself out of trouble," he observed.

Autumn let out a soft snort. "I am, but I've never had to put it to the test."

"Look, I'll see if I can find out more about the security systems, but I can't promise anything. How long have you got?"

"I need to retrieve it tomorrow."

"Then you're a fool. You're never going to be able to pull that off."

She didn't necessarily think he was wrong, but there was definitely a part of her that was more convinced than ever to steal the diadem just to prove she could.

She squashed that part down. If she lost her objectivity, then she'd end up caught.

"Thanks for your information." She set a small wad of cash on the bar. "Enjoy your drink."

She slid off her seat and turned away, leaving her drink untouched. She could choose to drink it and not let the alcohol affect her, but she was never sure how much she actually trusted that paranormal trick.

"Be careful," Desmond said.

"You shouldn't worry about me," she responded.

"It's not you I'm trying to protect, it's my business." Despite the dismissiveness of his words, she could sense the edge of genuine concern in them.

"I will be." She didn't wait for him to say anything else and headed out the door. She had a plan to make, and she couldn't afford to waste any time.

CHAPTER 12

NATHAIR

I t was surprisingly easy for Nathair to find the flat Autumn had sent him to. Perhaps that shouldn't have surprised him considering that she'd given him the address, but this was Autumn. He wouldn't have been surprised if there were several highly dangerous tasks required in order to gain entry. There still could be.

Nerves fluttered within him as he approached the front door. What if she'd changed her mind about him coming to join her? She might not need him anymore if she'd found a way to get out of the marriage situation herself.

He pushed the thoughts aside. He trusted Autumn, even if he didn't know why. She wasn't about to turn him away after inviting him here.

Nathair knocked calmly on the door and stepped back to wait.

It swung open almost straight away to reveal the dark-haired dryad on the other side.

His heart skipped a beat the moment she smiled at him.

"You found me," she said, gesturing for him to come inside, hesitating slightly as if she wanted to greet him in a slightly different way.

"You give good instructions," he responded.

"I gave you an address," she countered.

"Which counts as good."

She frowned, as if considering that he was right for the first time. "I suppose that's true. Do you want a drink?"

He shook his head. "Maybe in a bit."

"The kitchen's through there, if you change your mind at any point." She waved to the exit on the other side of the room. "The bedroom and bathroom are down there." She pointed to a corridor with two doors off it.

"Bedroom?"

She blushed in a way that didn't seem much like her, but did at the same time. "Sorry, there's only one. You can sleep on the bed if you prefer it to the sofa. Or we can..." She trailed off.

"We can?"

Autumn took a deep breath, while indicating that the two of them should take a seat on the sofa. "I was going to say we can share, but then I realised how it sounds."

"And how does it sound?"

"Presumptuous. Especially after we kissed."

"Do you think it was a mistake?" he asked.

She shook her head. "No."

"Then why is it a bad thing?"

"I don't know how you felt. Normally, I wouldn't care, but this time feels different."

He nodded. "I know what you mean."

She sighed and glanced down at her hands as she fiddled with what looked like a bracelet made of some kind of wood.

Which reminded him that he was supposed to give her a piece of her tree. He pulled it out of his pocket and held it out to her.

She looked up, surprised. "Thank you." She took it from him and let out a loud sigh. "That's better," she admitted.

"What is?" The question slipped from him before he thought about whether or not he should be asking it.

"I can't be away from my tree for too long, but having a piece of it with me helps. It'll only keep me going for a day or two at the most, but that's enough for what we need."

"What happens if you don't get back to your tree in time?" he asked.

"I get sick. It isn't a nice feeling and I'd rather avoid it if at all possible. It certainly won't make stealing the diadem very easy."

"Do you have a plan for getting it?" He didn't like the idea of stealing anything from anyone. Even a museum who probably shouldn't have it in the first place, but that didn't mean he wasn't going to do it. Not with what was on the line. Autumn's freedom was worth twisting a few laws over

"Sort of," she admitted. "But we can talk about that later."

He raised an eyebrow, unsure why she'd want to put off the reason they were both here.

"I want to go back to talking about that kiss."

"Oh." He liked *that.* "Anything in particular about it?"

She bit her bottom lip, making him more aware of the event she was talking about.

"I know it was only short, but I've never felt like that before," she admitted. "It was like it was something more than a kiss. Does that make sense?"

"Perfectly," he agreed.

"I think we're mates," she said. "I've been thinking about it, and that explanation seems to be the one that fits together. We're meant to be with one another, so of course our kiss felt that way. It was like finding the other half of me."

He grinned widely. "Is there a way to find out for sure?"

"Yes." The word was barely audible.

"What does it involve? We could do it now."

Autumn coughed, spluttering slightly as she regained her composure. He wasn't sure what he'd suggested to cause a reaction like that in her.

"Sex," she responded. "It involves us having sex."

"Ah." That explained the reaction, though he was a little hurt that she was so against the idea. "And you don't want to?"

"What? No. I'm sorry, I didn't mean to make you feel like I didn't. Your phrasing caught me off guard," she responded.

He stared at her, trying to make sense of what was happening.

Autumn shuffled along the sofa, bringing the two of them surprisingly close together.

"I'd like it if you kissed me again," she said in a low voice. "And if you want to go further, then I'd like that too."

A bolt of desire shot through him at the thought of sharing a more intimate moment with Autumn.

"Are you sure we have time before we go get the diadem?" he asked, not wanting to compromise what they came for, even if it was for a good reason

She nodded, seeming to understand what his delay was about. "We can't do anything until tomorrow anyway."

"Then we should enjoy tonight." He leaned closer to her, noticing she'd already come within touching distance.

"That sounds like a plan to me."

He wasn't sure which of them made the first move, but Autumn's lips were on his and she pressed herself against his.

He threaded his hand into his hair and pulled her closer, desperate for more than just a taste of her.

Nathair didn't need anything else to know the truth. They were mates. He could feel it all the way down to his core. Autumn was his mate.

And he was going to spend his whole life treasuring her. But for now, he was going to focus on making it clear how much he wanted her.

CHAPTER 13

AUTUMN

They broke apart, leaving Autumn breathing almost uncomfortably fast. There was a need inside her that she'd never felt before, and she wanted nothing more than to fulfil the need and take him through to the other room.

She paused for a moment, realising there was nothing stopping her unless he didn't want to.

Autumn cleared her throat. "Would you like to go to the other room?" Her voice came out low and husky, revealing how much need she'd built up for him during their one kiss.

"Are you sure?" Nathair replied, his gaze searching hers for the answer to his question.

"If you are."

His lips quirked up into a smile. "I've never been more sure of anything," he admitted.

She got to her feet and held out her hand. He took it instantly, and she guided him in the direction of the flat's only bedroom. Right now, she was glad it only had one. She led him inside and turned to face him, a little unsure of what to do now.

Nathair didn't have the same questions, and tugged on her hand to draw her closer.

Their lips crushed together once more and he kissed her with a reckless abandon that set her entire body on fire. She'd never had this response to anyone, and she knew she wouldn't again. This was a sensation that was unique to the two of them, and couldn't be matched.

After all, what was the point of having a fated mate if someone else could make you feel the same?

They barely broke their kiss as they tore at one another's clothes, sending them cascading to the floor in a ragged heap. Autumn didn't care. They'd pick them up in the morning, it wouldn't do any harm to leave them there.

She pulled away from his kisses and laid back on the bed. Nathair's gaze raked over her naked body, leaving a trail of heat in its path.

"I have a question," she asked, her voice soft and full of need.

"Hmm?" He climbed onto the bed beside her.

"I'm not sure how to ask it."

"With words?" he suggested.

"Don't be a smartass."

"You can ask me anything," he promised.

She bit her bottom lip, wondering what the best way to ask this was. "It's about your tongue."

Nathair frowned. "What about it?"

"Is it...forked?"

He raised an eyebrow. "That isn't the question I expected."

"Well? Is it?"

He stuck out his tongue so she could see, only to find herself disappointed by the humanness of it. "Do you want it to be?" he asked.

"I don't know."

A salacious grin spread over his features. "Do you want to find out?" There was a slight hiss at the end of his words, and it took her a moment to realise what he'd done.

A wave of desire flooded through her at the thought. She nodded, eager to see what he had in store.

He leaned in and pressed his lips against her neck, the soft caress nothing compared to the anticipation it brought. Even if the feel of the forked tongue was disappointing, it was worth it for the anticipation it was building inside her. She'd never wanted anyone or anything as much as she wanted this.

His lips parted and his tongue darted against her skin, tickling in a way she hadn't expected.

He repeated the same movements down her neck and across her collarbone, causing the most exquisite sensations she'd ever experienced. The moment his tongue flicked over her nipples, she let out a small cry, unable to contain her excitement.

She felt Nathair smile against her skin, clearly satisfied with the reaction he'd caused.

He moved his attention to her other breast, while his hand skimmed down her stomach. He didn't waste any time slipping it between her legs to let his fingers trail against her entrance. No doubt he could feel the effect he was having on her, which only seemed to heighten his satisfaction.

Slowly, he pushed his finger inside her. Autumn let out a small moan, unable to hold it back.

Nathair took it as a sign to move on and start his exploration of her stomach. The angle meant he had to remove his fingers, but she wasn't able to mourn their loss for too long. Not when she could tell what was going to happen next.

He settled between her legs and looked up at her, his gaze meeting hers. She could tell from the way it bore into her that he wanted her to watch. He wanted her to know what he was doing to her.

His tongue darted out, slimmer than it had been before and split into two elegant prongs. Even the sight of it was enough to cause a pulse of desire.

She wasn't going to last long.

Nathair lapped against her, his tongue tickling and teasing in a way she hadn't expected. He slid his fingers back inside her and curled them upwards, sending her desire curling up within her. She wasn't going to be able to hold it back much longer, nor did she really want to.

Autumn threaded her fingers through his hair and tugged ever so slightly in response to his movements. She wasn't exactly urging him on, but nor was she not.

Her whole body tensed and began to shudder, sending her crashing over the edge of her release. She cried out, but wasn't able to tell precisely what she was saying.

Nathair didn't let up. Instead, he prolonged her pleasure, making it impossible to escape and all the more delicious for it.

Slowly, she came back to her senses, both sated and eager for more in a way she'd never been before.

"Nate," she whispered, her voice hoarse from her cries.

He broke away from what he was doing and he looked up at her with concern in his eyes. "Is everything okay?"

"More than," she promised. "But I want you."

"You can have me," he promised, climbing up so their bodies were next to one another again.

She reached out and cupped his cheek in her hand, pulling him to her and pressing her lips against his. He'd shifted his tongue back to his human form, but she could still taste herself on him.

She placed a hand on his shoulder and pushed him back so he was lying on the bed. She swung her leg over him and reached down so she could guide him into her.

They fit perfectly. He filled her in just the right way and it made her want him more. Slowly, she began to move in a steady rhythm, connecting the two of them in a new way.

It was easy to lose herself in the power of the moment, and they were soon moving in perfect unison.

Nathair sat up, only causing him to seat himself deeper within her. She let out a loud moan, wanting more.

"I want to bite you," he whispered.

"That's okay."

"Is it not strange?" His words were broken by the shallow breaths and soft moans.

"It's normal," she promised, her own voice sounding similar to his. "It's the mating bond."

"Oh." His surprise was real, but it was enough to assure him that what he wanted was real and normal.

He kissed her neck before opening his mouth and letting his teeth graze her skin.

Autumn let out a small groan and exposed more of her neck so he could bite her. She'd never thought about this part before, but now she was in the moment, she wanted nothing more than to feel his teeth sinking through her skin and sealing them together for the rest of their lives.

The moment it happened, her whole world shrank and stars popped in front of her eyes. Another release had been building, but this was enough to send her catapulting over the edge.

She was vaguely aware of him falling over it with her, joining her in a moment only the two of them could share.

Once she was spent, she fell back onto the bed with Nathair beside them. A thin sheen of sweat covered her body, and the glow deep within her could have been enough to light a fire.

Nathair stroked her cheek gently, gazing at her with an intensity she'd never seen before. "That wasn't what I expected," he admitted.

"Me neither. But then again, I've never slept with my mate before." A wide smile spread over her face. "It's not something I'd mind doing again though."

Nathair let out a light laugh. "I'd hope you wouldn't, it's something I'd like to repeat."

"Maybe we should have something to eat and then we could spend the rest of the evening in bed?" she suggested. "We can't do anything until tomorrow evening anyway, so we can plan during the day and just enjoy tonight?"

"That sounds good to me," he promised.

Relief washed through her. She wasn't normally the kind to push a mission to the side, but in this case, she wanted one night where she didn't have to think about it. Tonight could just be about the two of them and nothing else.

Thankfully, he seemed to have no problem with that. Which meant she might get to do some exploring with her own tongue.

She pushed the wicked thoughts aside, but not too far. After all, she'd have use for them once they'd gotten something to eat.

CHAPTER 14

NATHAIR

N athair couldn't keep his eyes off the beautiful dryad standing over schematic layouts of the museum they were supposed to be breaking into. No matter how much he tried, he couldn't rid himself of thoughts from the night before. Not when it had been a connection unlike any he'd experienced before.

Just a few weeks ago, he'd wondered whether he even had a mate. Now he was sitting in the same room as his, having sealed their bond and given into something so powerful he knew he couldn't resist.

No wonder genies were unable to recreate this kind of bond. It felt stronger than any magic his family had ever performed. Perhaps he'd ask about it once he got home. He hadn't told either of his parents about

Autumn yet, but that was going to change once they'd sorted out their more immediate problem.

"How often have you done things like this?" he asked, only a little concerned about how well prepared Autumn seemed to be.

She flashed him a wry smile. "Stolen things for myself? This is the first time. Stolen something from a museum? A few times. Though never an item this big or valuable. And my work mostly takes me to the homes of private collectors. They tend to have very different security setups."

He blinked a couple of times while he tried to make sense of what she was saying. "What exactly is your job?" He wasn't sure whether it was his curiosity or his concern that came across more.

"I retrieve stolen goods for people who want them found," she told him.

"So you steal stolen stuff?"

"I mean, you could put it like that, but it's not what I put on my tax return."

He chuckled. "Then what do you put?"

"*Retrieval Specialist.*"

Nathair snorted. "Is that really so much better?"

"I assume so, no one has ever actually asked me what it means. I take that as a good sign."

"What happens if someone reports the things you steal as stolen?" he asked.

"I'll tell you when it happens. In most cases, they won't because they stole the item in the first place. It's not like you can report something you don't have legally to the police. It raises questions you don't want to have answered."

"I hadn't thought of it that way."

"I didn't either at first. I always just thought I was getting lucky that no one wanted to report anything I stole. It wasn't until someone pointed it out that I realised what an idiot I'd been."

"I don't think I'd have thought about that either."

Autumn shrugged. "I don't suppose it matters. I understand how it works now. It's one of the reasons I make all of my clients prove that they're the rightful owner beyond any doubt. I don't want to get caught up in a legal situation where I can actually get caught stealing."

"Have you ever had someone employ you to steal something you already stole?"

She chuckled. "You're full of questions."

"I'm intrigued," he admitted. "I've been a gardener my entire life, this is all very exciting for me."

"Perhaps if you enjoy retrieving the diadem with me we could go into business together," she suggested. "It can be a lot of fun."

"And a little more dangerous than pruning a tree."

"I'm not so sure, have you never had one of the trees fight back? They can be a prickly bunch."

Nathair snorted. "I suppose you aren't wrong there."

"I rarely am," she teased. "But to answer your question, yes. But only once, and they ghosted me as soon as I asked them to prove the item belonged to them. I put some feelers out, but as far as I know, they didn't hire anyone else to do the job either, and the rightful owner still has it in their possession."

"Does your father know this is what you do?"

She gave a bitter laugh, giving him all the answer he needed.

"He doesn't even know I have a job. Though I think he suspects. But I had to do something. At first, it was about the boredom. But after a while, it became about the future independence. I thought that if I saved up enough money, I'd be able to leave home and never look back."

"What about your tree?" He remembered her saying that she wasn't able to go far from it. If that was the case, then it wouldn't be possible for her to just leave home.

"That's the problem with my plan," she admitted. "But I carried on because I figured that one day I'd come up with an answer."

"Have you?"

"No. Though you might change that."

"Me?"

She nodded. "Felix told me that he stopped needing his tree the same way once he was mated to Mia. She's a witch, not a dryad, so I think the mating bond does something to the bond with our plants. It doesn't weaken it as such, but gives it an alternative path. I'm not sure exactly how it works, I'm not someone who understands genes or DNA or all that other sciency stuff."

"There are people working on that?"

"Mmhmm. Somewhere."

"Huh." He'd never thought about that. Could someone like that unlock the secrets of why he was able to become human? He wasn't about to search them out. The last thing he wanted was to become a science specimen, but it would certainly be an interesting thing to discover.

"Anyway, come check these out. I need to know if you think you'll be able to climb through a grate."

"It depends if there's anything for me to coil around to get up there," he admitted. "But it should be possible."

He got to his feet and made his way over to her.

She pointed to a section on the map and he leaned over to study it, only realising after that he had no idea what he was looking at. "I've never seen anything like this before," he told her.

"Ah. Right. Okay, so this is the room where the diadem is being kept. We can't get into it the normal way because there is more security around the doors. So I was thinking we could get in through this system here." She pointed to a thin line running all along the map.

"What is it?"

She shrugged. "No idea. The building is old, so there are lots of things like this that aren't used anymore. It's helpful for us, a nightmare for building upkeep."

"And you need me to go up here?"

She nodded. "From what I can gather, it's big enough for a person up to here." She pointed to the corner of the room. "I think this is an escape tunnel from before it became a museum, but no one has ever thought to block it off. The only problem is that it's going to be locked from the outside."

"Which is where I come in?"

"Yes. You can shift with your clothes on, right?"

He nodded.

"Huh, I bet a lot of shifters would love that ability."

"Can shifters not do that?"

"No. It's one of the things they complain about the most, especially if they've had a few drinks and let the alcohol worm it's way into their system."

"I never realised."

"It's handy for us, otherwise you'd have to leave your clothes hanging around while you shifted. And while I do enjoy seeing you naked, I'm not sure it's the best thing for our plan."

"Probably not," he agreed.

"Can you take items with you when you shift? If they're in your pockets?"

"Yes. The magic seems to cover anything that's on my person and not living."

"This just gets better and better. In which case, you can take a lock picking kit..."

"I can't pick locks."

"Then it's a good job we have time to teach you."

He watched her head over to a suitcase and pulled out a small box. He frowned, confused about what that might have to do with lock picking until she set it down in front of him.

"Lock picking one-o-one," she announced, picking up the fake lock and putting it in front of him. "You're going to pick this up in no time."

He hoped beyond anything that she was right.

CHAPTER 15

AUTUMN

T here was nothing like the few moments of calm before a heist began. She loved the way it felt. The tension had already set in, and the plans were already laid. It was the calm before the storm, and it was almost as good as the way it felt to have gotten out with the item in her backpack.

Except this time felt different, though it wasn't because Nathair was with her. In fact, that was adding to the excitement. She had someone to share the experience with, and that was fun.

The diadem itself was the problem, and not because it was going to be more of a challenge to steal than some of her other missions. She just didn't like that she was stealing it for herself. Technically, the diadem should belong to the nymphs and shouldn't be locked away in a glass museum display case, but they hadn't been the ones to contract her to get it. She was doing this for selfish reasons, and that wasn't good.

Maybe after all of this was over, she'd find a way to steal the diadem back from her father and return it to the museum.

Except that wouldn't be the right answer either. It didn't belong here.

She pushed her thoughts aside. Now wasn't the right time to be thinking about the future. Her only job was to focus on the present and getting both them and the diadem out safely.

"You should shift," she whispered to Nathair. "It'll make you harder to spot."

"What about you?" he asked.

Smug satisfaction came over her. "Watch."

She let her magic flow through her veins and stepped back into the shadows. From the expression on Nathair's face, it had precisely the desired effect and had allowed her to blend seamlessly into the background. Dryad magic wasn't particularly strong unless she was tending to a plant, but the one thing it was handy for in the outside world was disappearing into the shadows without being seen.

"Just a trick of the trade," she quipped as she let the effect wear off.

"I'm sure that would sound a lot more impressive if I wasn't aware magic existed," Nathair responded.

"Perhaps, but it was fun anyway. If you shift, I'll carry you and then neither of us will be seen."

He nodded and purple smoke filled the air, swirling around him and transforming back into the small golden snake she'd met several times before.

She scooped him up and put him in her pocket, trying not to think about how weird it was to do something like that to her mate. If they did this more often, then perhaps she'd get used to it. She could see how his shifting abilities might give her an edge in certain jobs.

Autumn pulled her magic to the forefront again and disappeared into the shadows. It didn't make her invisible, but it would make it so that she was hard to spot, particularly for people who didn't know to look for her.

"We're entering now." She felt a little silly about talking to her pocket, but she didn't want to leave Nathair in the dark about what they were doing. This was his first heist, which meant she needed to keep him in the loop.

She pulled the creaky old door back and headed inside the passageway. She was lucky the museum owners had overlooked it whenever they did renovations or this would be a lot harder than it should be. Fortunately for her, these kinds of entries were often ignored, even by security. It made her job a lot easier.

The ground was soft under her feet, making Autumn wonder how long it had been since the last person walked the same way. It couldn't have been too long given the lack of cobwebs. Hopefully, she wasn't going to run into anyone patrolling the corridors.

She got to the end in the right amount of time, reassuring herself that she'd read the plans correctly and wasn't about to get the two of them caught.

"It's your turn now," she said to Nathair, helping him out of her pocket and reaching up to the grate at the top of the room.

He hissed and nodded his head, slithering through and heading out the other side.

Autumn's heart pounded as she waited for him to slither through the grate and unlocked the door on her other side. It was hard to give such an important part of the mission to someone else, but she wasn't against using the tools she had at her disposal, and that included using other people's skills.

She didn't relax until there was a loud clunk and the door in front of her swung open, revealing a smiling Nathair on the other side.

"It went just like you said."

"I hope you're not surprised," Autumn responded. "There's a reason I'm good at what I do."

"I have no doubt about that."

"Make sure you shift the moment there seems to be trouble. No one will notice you in your snake form."

"i]I've already got it," he promised. "You made me repeat the plan several times already."

"I'm sorry. I'm not used to having a partner when I do things like this."

He nodded, seeming to understand. "We leave the door open, right?" he asked.

She nodded. "It's worth the risk to be able to make a swift getaway. If someone is in the room enough to see the door is open, then they've probably already worked out that we're in the room."

"Makes sense," he agreed.

She had to admit being impressed by how well Nathair was taking instructions. A lot of people in his position would fight against her instructions.

"All right, keep your eyes peeled, but it should be fairly straightforward from here on."

"This hasn't been very difficult," he observed.

She chuckled. "I often find that's the case. It surprises me that more security firms don't employ paranormals to make sure museums and big houses actually have adequate security."

"It would probably help if they knew we existed," Nathair pointed out.

"Hmm, true."

She led him through the room, being careful to avoid the cameras directed at the most important items. From experience, she knew there probably wouldn't be someone manning them all the time, and if there was, they wouldn't be paying much attention unless they already knew someone was in the building.

Yet another thing that was going to make their jobs easier.

"Wait." She shot out an arm to stop Nathair from stepping onto a floor tile that was supposed to have a pressure sensor on it. "We need to go around that one."

"How do you know?"

"I memorised the plans before we left."

He blinked a couple of times, conveying his confusion despite the fact she couldn't see more of his face.

"I do it every time," she explained. "It makes it easier."

"I don't doubt that, I'm just impressed you can commit them to memory."

"Oh." Thankfully, her ski mask covered the blush that rose to her cheeks. "Come on, you should be okay if you follow me."

She moved quickly through the room, avoiding any of the other tiles she thought would be triggered if they stepped on them.

It only took a couple of minutes for them to reach the case with the diadem sitting on the dark blue velvet.

"It's not what I expected it to be," Nathair admitted.

"Because it's not made of a precious metal?"

He nodded. "I expected it to glitter."

"Gems and metals aren't important to the Nymph Council. They want to celebrate the gifts nature gives us."

"Don't precious stones and metals come from the ground?"

"They do," she agreed. "I didn't say it made sense, just that it was how the nymphs worked."

"It does sound rather backwards."

"Mmhmm. But then again, we're trying to steal a diadem because Dad wants to marry me off," she pointed out.

"That's fair."

"Do you have the device I gave you?" she asked.

Nathair dug his hand into his pocket and pulled out a small device that looked like a digital clock.

At one point in its life, it had been, but the witch Autumn had bought it off had done some tinkering, both with the mechanics and magically.

"Thanks." She took it from him and placed it on the control panel of the diadem's podium. She punched in a code to activate it and stepped back.

"How does it work?" Nathair asked.

"Is it bad if I said I had no idea? A witch made it for me and explained how it worked, and that's all I ever needed to know. It's probably a modification the Witch Council wouldn't approve of, so I operated on his don't-ask-don't-tell policy."

A soft beeping came from the machine, followed by a click as the glass door swung open.

Nathair let out a low whistle. "Impressive."

Autumn chuckled. "Right? It's one of the gadgets I'd replace straight away if it broke. Do you have the bag?"

He handed her a soft velvet pouch.

"Are you sure this will shift with you if you put it in your pocket?" she asked.

"I've never found anything that wouldn't. But there's a first time for everything."

"All right, maybe we should try it so we know." She had no problem carrying the contraband out of the building herself, but it would be a lot better if Nathair could do it in his shifted form, especially as that would make it impossible for anyone who caught them to find the diadem.

She reached into the case and picked up the diadem, confident that the witch-made device had disabled all of the remaining safety measures. She slipped it into the velvet bag and handed it back to Nathair.

He placed it in his pocket and before she'd even asked, the purple smoke which signalled a shift plumed up around him.

Autumn held her breath, hoping the diadem would transform with him. It would be a handy trick if Nathair came with her on more trips like this one.

"It's looking good," she said unnecessarily.

Nathair's snake form nodded at her. Or she assumed he did. She had no idea how much thinking he was able to do in snake-form, or if he was limited. She knew shifters mostly retained their human consciousness, but she'd never met anyone like Nathair before. Would being born as a reptile make him different?

She doubted so. If they were fated mates, then that implied he was a normal paranormal. Or at least as normal as paranormals got.

She pushed the thoughts out of her head. Now wasn't the time to think about them. And it would be better if she *talked* to him rather than assuming anything. She was sure he'd tell her.

Footsteps sounded from the other room, making her freeze. She hadn't thought any of the guards were going to find them, but it seemed as if she was wrong. They must have taken too long.

"I'm going to pick you up," she told Nathair.

He nodded again.

She took a deep breath and scooped him off the ground, placing him carefully into her pocket. This was the best way to make use of both of their abilities. He was small enough that he could be hidden in her clothing, along with the diadem, and she could slink into the shadows and not be seen unless someone was right in front of her.

Carefully, she made her way around the corner of the room. Her heart pounded, and she worried it would give her away despite knowing that wasn't likely. Even if the guard was paranormal, which was unlikely, he'd have to have exceptionally good hearing to make it out.

She paused when she was a few feet away from the open door, wanting to be sure that the guard wasn't about to turn the corner and spot her. While she could make herself disappear into the shadows, there wasn't much she could do about an open door.

Once she was satisfied they weren't about to be caught, she slipped through the entrance and down the passage to freedom.

She didn't look back until they were several streets away, and only then it was to be sure they weren't being followed before they headed back to the flat.

She hadn't gotten the reputation she had by being sloppy when it mattered. And this wasn't going to be the job she got caught on.

CHAPTER 16

NATHAIR

Nathair could sense how unhappy Autumn was, even if he couldn't understand exactly what the problem was, they'd gotten the diadem successfully, and now she'd be able to marry who she wanted.

And yet here she was pacing up and down in front of the entrance to her father's room.

"What's wrong?" he asked.

She let out a long drawn out sigh. "I don't know," she admitted. "It's just that I thought I'd feel better right now. We've got the diadem and I don't have to marry Rylan, but somehow I don't feel like I'm in control."

"That's because I have this." He held out the diadem for her.

"Because you need to give it to Dad so he can pronounce this entire thing as over."

"I think you should give it to him," Nathair responded.

"Nate..."

"I know that wasn't technically the mission, but I think it's the only way you'll ever be happy. I don't want you to be forced to marry me any more than I want you to be forced to marry Rylan."

A small smile spread over Autumn's face, letting him know that he'd done the right thing. While he'd been reasonably sure she'd take the diadem, a small part of him had worried that she wouldn't.

"Thank you." She leaned in and kissed his cheek. "Do you want to come in with me?" She gestured to the door.

"Not really, but I will anyway."

Autumn chuckled. "I know the feeling. I'd rather not go inside either," she admitted.

"But it's the only way to end things."

"Exactly." She let out a long sigh. "All right, wish me luck."

"You don't need it," he pointed out. "But you have it anyway."

"Smooth," she muttered. "I'm ready when you are."

"Same here."

Slowly, she pushed open the door and strode into her father's study. Nathair trailed behind, unsure what he should be doing with himself in this situation. This was Autumn's moment, he was just here to support her.

Hopefully, she knew that.

"Autumn, what are you doing here?" her father asked.

"I brought you this," she responded firmly, placing the diadem on his desk. "I've fulfilled the challenge and now have the right to choose not to marry."

"That wasn't the deal," her father said.

"It is now. I won't be marrying Rylan."

Anger flitted over his face.

"And before you argue, you should know that I've found my fated mate, and it's not the man you want me to marry."

Surprise flitted across the older man's face while Nathair shifted back and forth with nerves. He knew the dryad's attention would turn to him soon.

"Why have you never said? I'd never have insisted on you marrying Rylan if I'd known." Something in the older man's voice convinced Nathair that he was telling the truth. Perhaps this had been nothing more than a misguided attempt to secure his daughter's happiness.

Autumn sighed. "Because I didn't meet him until your competition had started. This is Nathair." She gestured to him and he stepped forward.

If anything, Autumn's father looked more surprised than ever. "Weren't you taking part in the marriage competition?"

"I was, sir," Nathair responded.

"And you're my daughter's mate?"

"I am." He crossed his hands behind his back and stood up as straight as possible, hoping it made a good impression on his new father-in-law.

"Why were you taking part in the competition if you're her mate?"

"I was competing for Autumn," he said. "So that she could have the choice about who she married. I didn't realise she was my mate when I first met her." He didn't add that he hadn't even been sure he had a mate. That information was for Autumn only.

Autumn's father sighed loudly and turned to his daughter. "I'm sorry," he said.

Nathair tried to keep his surprise off his face, but he wasn't sure he managed. Thankfully, Autumn's father seemed to have stopped paying attention to him now.

"Apology accepted," Autumn responded. "I take it you don't need anything else from us?"

He shook his head.

"Good. I'll see you tomorrow." She turned around and walked past Nathair, grabbing his hand as she did.

He had no idea what she was up to, but he knew the best thing to do was to go along with it, especially if it got him more alone time with Autumn.

She led him out of the room and back out into the huge house.

"Where are we going?" he asked

"To celebrate." Her lips curved up into a knowing smile, and it only took him a moment to realise what she meant.

"In which case, I'm all yours."

Autumn laughed lightly. "I was hoping you'd say that."

She didn't stop until they reached a door up the stairs. While he didn't know for certain what was on the other side, he certainly hoped it would be her bedroom so they could spend some time alone. While they'd had their night together in the flat, it had been overshadowed by the knowledge of what they needed to do the next day.

Now, they'd be able to take their time.

Autumn pushed it open and stepped inside, dragging him with her. The moment they were inside, she pushed him against the wall and captured his lips with hers.

His body responded instantly. He needed her more than he'd ever needed anyone before, and it seemed like she felt the same.

Her fingers quickly undid the buttons of his shirt and he twisted so he could shrug it off easier, longing for the feel of her hands running over his chest. Autumn broke away from their kiss, making him want to grab her and pull her back.

But she seemed to have other ideas. She looked up at him with a small smile on her face and a devious twinkle in her eye.

Nathair had no idea what she had planned, all he knew was that he was going to enjoy every moment of it.

CHAPTER 17

AUTUMN

D espite the fact she'd barely started with her plans, Nathair already seemed to be in a daze. Now it was down to Autumn to show him just how good it could get.

She sank to her knees and unbuttoned his fly, keeping her gaze locked with his. He stiffened as he properly realised what she was going to do, which made her feel more powerful than ever.

She stripped off the rest of his clothes, leaving him naked and proud before her. She licked her lips.

"Autumn," he said.

"Mmhmm?"

"You don't have to do this."

"I know. But I want to." She reached out and took him in her hand, stroking him gently.

He let out a loud groan and tipped his head back, only spurring her on further.

Slowly, she guided him into her mouth, letting him fill her.

Nathair let out a loud gasp, his hands coming down and threading into her hair. He didn't try to control her movements. Instead, it was more about the connection it created between the two of them.

She began to move, taking more of him. She swirled her tongue around him, gaining another round of moans from him. All she could focus on was giving him pleasure.

"Autumn, you're going to have to stop," he said, the words punctured by shallow pants. He gently pushed on her shoulders.

She moved away, not wanting to push him further than he wanted to.

"Is everything all right?" she asked.

He smiled reassuringly at her. "It definitely is."

"Then why..."

Before she could finish her question, he leaned down and scooped her off her feet, carrying her over to the bed. "If you carried on, then we'd have had to stop."

"Oh." Somehow, she hadn't considered that.

The moment he set her down, she took matters into her own hands and stripped off her clothes. She had no problem being naked, especially with the intense way Nathair was staring at her.

She laid down on the bed and stretched out, loving the way Nathair raked his gaze over her.

He climbed onto the bed and leaned over her, capturing her lips with his. She arched her back and pushed her chest against his.

He slipped his fingers between them and trailed them up the inside of her thigh. She moaned into his mouth, desperate for him to touch her.

"More," she whispered.

He chuckled, the sound vibrating through her.

The moment he pushed his fingers inside her, she knew she wasn't going to last long. He curled them up, pressing against the spot that she knew would make her explode.

"Nate." She could barely get her words out over the intensity of the way he was making her feel. "I want all of you."

"Your wish is my command." He pulled his fingers from her, and she instantly missed them. Perhaps she shouldn't have asked for more yet after all.

In one smooth movement, he pushed himself into her.

Autumn closed her eyes and tipped her head back, enjoying the perfect way he filled her. No one had ever come close to making her feel the way Nathair did.

She clawed at his back, needing him closer, even if it was physically impossible. She lost herself in the steady rhythm of their bodies moving together.

Her release twisted and curled inside her, already threatening to explode from her at any moment.

She pushed it down, wanting to hold off for as long as possible. They'd have plenty of time to explore one another's bodies, but that didn't mean she was ready for this to end.

"Let go, Autumn," Nathair whispered in her ear.

He pushed deeper inside her, hitting the spot that made her scream out.

Her release followed, crashing over her in a wave and consuming every part of her. It was almost as if fireworks were exploding in her mind, stopping any rational thought.

Nathair's pace quickened as he reached his release, which only prolonged her own.

Completely spent, she collapsed back onto the bed with Nathair beside her.

Once she'd recovered some of her breath, she rolled over and placed her head on his shoulder. Nathair stroked her back gently. His touch was so tender, she never wanted it to end.

"It's never been like that before," she whispered.

"I know what you mean," he responded. "I guess we'll have the rest of our lives to get used to it."

It took a moment for the meaning of his words to sink in. She already knew that mating was for life, and that she wouldn't want to change that, but she hadn't really considered what that would mean.

"Thank you for helping me with my father," she said. "I know he's not easy to deal with."

"He wasn't so bad."

"That's because you haven't been properly introduced to our family life," she warned. "There's plenty of crazy coming."

He chuckled. "I think having to compete to be able to marry you was a good introduction."

She let out a small groan. "He's probably still going to want us to get married."

"I can think of worse fates," he teased.

Autumn laughed. "That's fair."

"So long as we can invite my family too."

"Absolutely. I can't wait to meet them."

"You're going to love them," he promised.

"I hope so." She'd never had to meet a boyfriend's parents before, mostly because they'd also been nymphs and she'd known them for her entire life. But this was different, and not just because he was her mate.

"Perhaps we could visit them tomorrow?" he suggested. "I know my parents will be excited to meet you."

"I'd like that. But what are we going to do until then?" she asked.

He raised an eyebrow. "I can think of a few things?"

"Care to enlighten me?"

"How about I show you instead?" he asked.

"I think I can be on board with that." Anticipation built inside her.

Nathair cupped her cheek in his hand and pulled her even closer.

His kiss transported her to another world, one that she never wanted to come back from.

She'd never really wanted to find her mate, but now that she had, she never wanted to let him go.

***

Thank you for reading *The Viper's Dream*, I hope you enjoyed it. If you want to continue *The Paranormal Council* series, you can with *The Tortoise's Race*: http://books2read.com/thetortoisesrace

If you want to read a bonus prologue for *The Viper's Dream* about Nathair turning from a snake

into   a   human,   you   can   find   it   here:
https://books.authorlauragreenwood.co.uk/rtbygulu
3c

AUTHOR NOTE

Thank you for reading *The Viper's Dream*, I hope you enjoyed it! And if you've been waiting since *Snakes and Ladders* released in 2018 for the conclusion to Autumn's story, thank you so much for your patience, and I hope it was everything you wanted it to be.

I never intended for it to take so long for Autumn and Nathair's story to be complete, but it was one of those that didn't make itself known for a while, and I didn't want to force it. I considered adding her story to at least three different series before realising its best home was in *The Paranormal Council* series (especially now that Felix and Mia's story, _The Hunter's Potion_, is part of the series too).

If you read *Snakes and Ladders*, you might have noticed some changes between that story and this one. I've gained a lot of writing experience since 2018 and I didn't feel like just continuing from the end of it would serve the series well. In this case, that meant incorporating some parts of the old story into the new one - hopefully, you'll agree that it's stronger for it!

If you want to keep up to date with new releases and other news, you can join my <u>Facebook Reader Group</u> or <u>mailing list</u>.

Stay safe & happy reading!

- Laura

Also by Laura Greenwood

Signed Paperback & Merchandise:

You can find signed paperbacks, hardcovers, and merchandise based on my series (including stickers, magnets, face masks, and more!) via my website: https://www.authorlauragreenwood.co.uk/p/shop.html

Series List:

* denotes a completed series

The Obscure World

- Ashryn Barker*

- Grimalkin Academy: Kittens*

- Grimalkin Academy: Catacombs*

- City Of Blood*

- Grimalkin Academy: Stakes*

- <u>Supernatural Retrieval Agency</u>*

- <u>The Black Fan</u>

- <u>Sabre Woods Academy</u>*

- <u>Scythe Grove Academy</u>*

- <u>The Shifter Season</u>

- <u>Cauldron Coffee Shop</u>

- <u>Obscure Academy</u>

- <u>Stonerest Academy</u>

- <u>Obscure World: Holidays</u>

The Forgotten Gods World

- <u>The Queen of Gods</u>*

- <u>Forgotten Gods</u>

- <u>Forgotten Gods: Origins</u>

The Grimm World

- <u>Grimm Academy</u>*

- <u>Fate Of The Crown</u>*

- <u>Once Upon An Academy Series</u>

- The Princess Competition

The Paranormal Council Universe

- The Paranormal Council Series

- The Fae Queen Of Winter Trilogy*

- Paranormal Criminal Investigations

- MatchMater Paranormal Dating App*

- The Necromancer Council*

- Return Of The Fae*

Other Series

- The Apprentice Of Anubis

- Beyond The Curse

- Untold Tales*

- The Dragon Duels*

- Rosewood Academy

- ME*

- Seven Wardens*, co-written with Skye MacKinnon

- <u>Tales Of Clan Robbins</u>, co-written with L.A. Boruff

- <u>Firehouse Witches</u>*, co-written with Lacey Carter Andersen & L.A. Boruff

- <u>Purple Oasis</u>, co-created series with Arizona Tape

Twin Souls Universe, all series co-written with
Arizona Tape

- <u>Twin Souls</u>*

- <u>Dragon Soul</u>*

- <u>The Renegade Dragons</u>*

- <u>The Vampire Detective</u>*

- <u>Amethyst's Wand Shop Mysteries</u>

- <u>The Necromancer Morgue Mysteries</u>

Mountain Shifters Universe, all series co-written with
L.A. Boruff

- <u>Valentine Pride</u>*

- <u>Magic and Metaphysics Academy</u>*

Audiobooks:

www.authorlauragreenwood.co.uk/p/audio.html

ABOUT THE AUTHOR

Laura is a USA Today Bestselling Author of paranormal, fantasy, urban fantasy, and contemporary romance. When she's not writing, she drinks a lot of tea, tries to resist French macarons, and works towards a diploma in Egyptology. She lives in the UK, where most of her books are set. Laura specialises in quick reads, whether you're looking for a swoonworthy romance for the bath, or an action-packed adventure for your latest journey, you'll find the perfect match amongst her books!

Follow the Author

- Website: www.authorlauragreenwood.co.uk

- Mailing   List: www.authorlauragreenwood.co.uk/p/mailing-list-sign-up.html

- Facebook Group: http://facebook.com/groups/theparanormalcounc il

- Facebook Page: http://facebook.com/authorlauragreenwood

- Bookbub: www.bookbub.com/authors/laura-greenwood

CPSIA information can be obtained
at www.ICGtesting.com
Printed in the USA
LVHW090813240122
709011LV00003BA/73

9 798201 267278